W9-ASP-011

RECEIVED 1989
OHIO DOMINICAN
LIBRARY
COLUMBUS OHIO

THE LITTLE DRUMMER BOY

Ezra Jack Keats

Words and Music by Katherine Davis,
Henry Onorati and Harry Simeone

SCHOLASTIC INC.
NEW YORK · TORONTO · LONDON · AUCKLAND · SYDNEY · TOKYO

J
K
c.2

No part of this publication may be reproduced in whole or in part, or stored in a retrieval system, or transmitted in any form or by any means, electronic, mechanical, photocopying, recording, or otherwise, without written permission of the publisher. For information regarding permission, write to Macmillan Publishing Co., Inc., 866 Third Avenue, New York, NY 10022.

ISBN 0-590-11868-4

Copyright © 1968 by Ezra Jack Keats. THE LITTLE DRUMMER BOY by H. Simeone, H. Onorati and K. Davis. Copyright © 1958 by Mills Music, Inc. and International Korwin Corp. Used by permission. All rights reserved. This edition is published by Scholastic Inc., 730 Broadway, New York, NY 10003, by arrangement with Macmillan Publishing Co.

18 17 16 15 14 13 12 11 10 9 8   4 5 6 7 8 9/8

Printed in the U.S.A.   07

THE LITTLE DRUMMER BOY

128926

Come, they told me,
(pa-rum-pum-pum-pum)

Our newborn King to see,
(pa-rum-pum-pum-pum)

Our finest gifts to bring
(*pa-rum-pum-pum-pum*)

To lay before the King,
(*pa-rum-pum-pum-pum, rum-pum-pum-pum, rum-pum-pum-pum*)

So to honor Him
(*pa-rum-pum-pum-pum*)

When we come.

Baby Jesus,
(pa-rum-pum-pum-pum)

I am a poor boy too,

(pa-rum-pum-pum-pum)

I have no gift to bring
(*pa-rum-pum-pum-pum*)

That's fit to give a king,
(*pa-rum-pum-pum-pum,*
rum-pum-pum-pum,
rum-pum-pum-pum)

Shall I play for you
(pa-rum-pum-pum-pum)

On my drum?

Mary nodded,
(pa-rum-pum-pum-pum)

The ox and lamb kept time,
(pa-rum-pum-pum-pum)

I played my drum for Him,
(pa-rum-pum-pum-pum)

I played my best for Him,
(pa-rum-pum-pum-pum,
rum-pum-pum-pum,
rum-pum-pum-pum)

Then He smiled at me,
(pa-rum-pum-pum-pum)

Me and my drum.

The Little Drummer Boy

Words and Music by KATHERINE DAVIS, HENRY ONORATI and HARRY SIMEONE

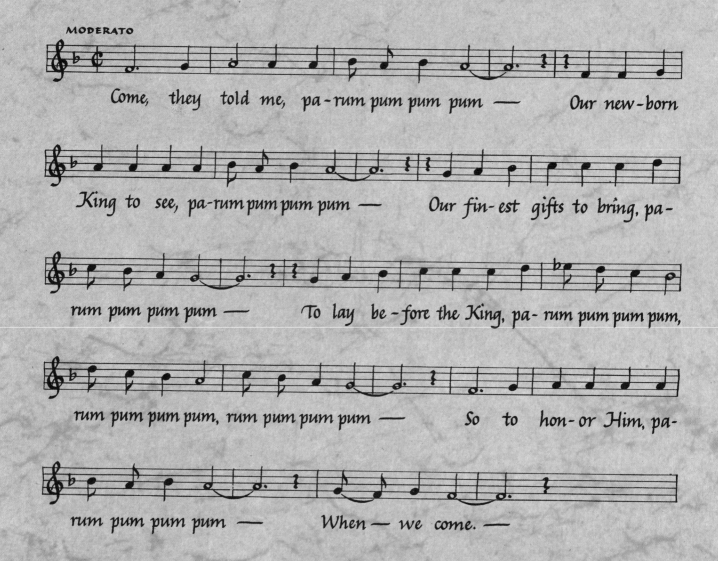

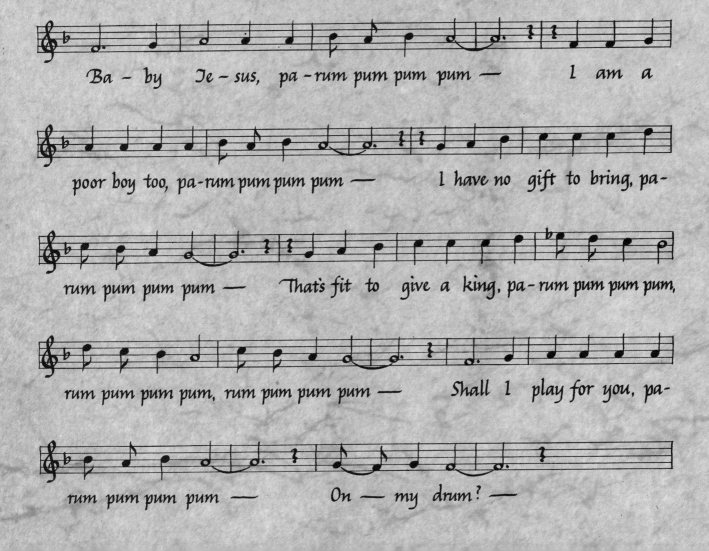

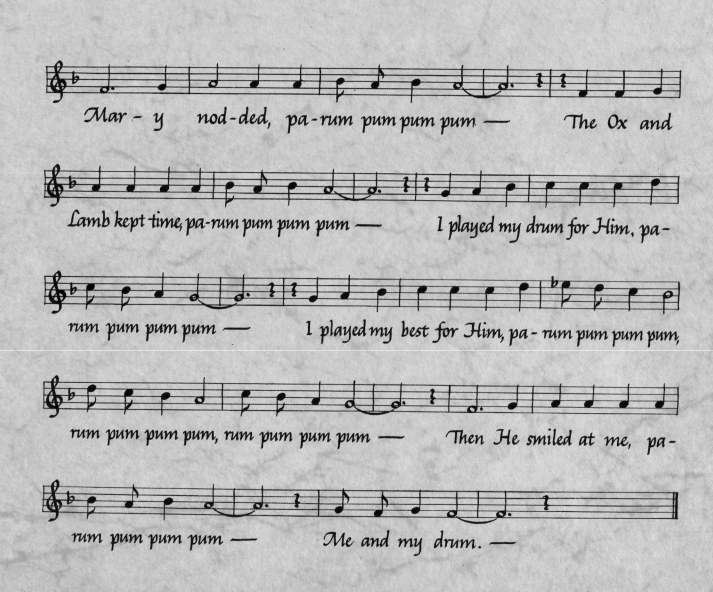